A P E R F E C T
▼ P R E S E N T

FOR _____

_____

FROM _____

_____ 19 _____

Illustrations © 1987 Michael McCurdy
Story Editor: Mary Dolan Delaney
Biographical Sketch: Susan C. Jones

Published by Redpath Press,
A Division of Redpath Associates, Inc.
420 North 5th Street, Suite 710
Minneapolis, Minnesota 55401

Printed in the United States
by Bolger Publications; Minneapolis, MN
Typesetting by Dix Type Inc.; Syracuse, NY

Acknowledgement: THE THREE FAT WOMEN OF ANTIBES
by W. Somerset Maugham from
THE COMPLETE SHORT STORIES OF W. SOMERSET MAUGHAM.
Copyright 1933 by W. Somerset Maugham.
Reprinted by permission of Doubleday & Company, Inc.
Copyright by the Royal Literary Fund.

Minneapolis, Minnesota
Redpath Press: 40 pages
ISBN 1-55628-022-X

W. SOMERSET MAUGHAM

THE THREE FAT WOMEN OF ANTIBES

INDULGE!

ILLUSTRATED BY
MICHAEL McCURDY

DESIGNED BY
RITA MARSHALL

REDPATH PRESS

THE THREE FAT
WOMEN OF ANTIBES

ONE WAS CALLED MRS RICHMAN AND she was a widow. The second was called Mrs Sutcliffe; she was American and she had divorced two husbands. The third was called Miss Hickson and she was a spinster. They were all in the comfortable forties and they were all well off. Mrs Sutcliffe had the odd first name of Arrow. When she was young and slender she had liked it well enough. It suited her and the jests it occasioned though too often repeated were very flattering; she was not disinclined to believe that it suited her character too: it suggested directness, speed, and purpose. She liked it less now that her delicate features had grown muzzy with fat, that her arms and shoulders were so substantial and her hips so massive. It was increasingly difficult to find dresses to make her look as she liked to look. The jests her name gave rise to now were made behind her back and she very well knew that they were far from obliging. But she was by no means resigned to middle age. She still wore blue to bring out the colour of her eyes and, with the help of art, her fair hair had kept its lustre. What she liked about Beatrice Richman and Frances Hickson was that they were both so much fatter than she, it made her look quite slim; they were both of them older and much inclined to treat her as a little young thing. It was not disagreeable. They were good-natured women and they chaffed her pleasantly about her beaux; they had both given up the thought of that kind of nonsense, indeed Miss Hickson had never given it a moment's consideration, but they were sympathetic to her flirtations. It was understood that one of these days Arrow would make a third man happy.

"Only you mustn't get any heavier, darling," said Mrs Richman.

"And for goodness' sake make certain of his bridge," said Miss Hickson.

They saw for her a man of about fifty, but well-preserved and of distin-

guished carriage, an admiral on the retired list and a good golfer, or a widower without encumbrances, but in any case with a substantial income. Arrow listened to them amiably, and kept to herself the fact that this was not at all her idea. It was true that she would have liked to marry again, but her fancy turned to a dark slim Italian with flashing eyes and a sonorous title or to a Spanish don of noble lineage; and not a day more than thirty. There were times when, looking at herself in her mirror, she was certain she did not look any more than that herself.

They were great friends, Miss Hickson, Mrs Richman, and Arrow Sutcliffe. It was their fat that had brought them together and bridge that had cemented their alliance. They had met first at Carlsbad, where they were staying at the same hotel and were treated by the same doctor who used them with the same ruthlessness. Beatrice Richman was enormous. She was a handsome woman, with fine eyes, rouged cheeks, and painted lips. She was very well content to be a widow with a handsome fortune. She adored her food. She liked bread and butter, cream, potatoes, and suet puddings, and for eleven months of the year ate pretty well everything she had a mind to, and for one month went to Carlsbad to reduce. But every year she grew fatter. She upbraided the doctor, but got no sympathy from him. He pointed out to her various plain and simple facts.

"But if I'm never to eat a thing I like, life isn't worth living," she expostulated.

He shrugged his disapproving shoulders. Afterwards she told Miss Hickson that she was beginning to suspect he wasn't so clever as she had thought. Miss Hickson gave a great guffaw. She was that sort of woman. She had a deep bass voice, a large flat sallow face from which twinkled little bright eyes; she walked with a slouch, her hands in her pockets, and when she could do so without exciting attention smoked a long cigar. She dressed as like a man as she could.

"What the deuce should I look like in frills and furbelows?" she said. "When you're as fat as I am you may just as well be comfortable."

She wore tweeds and heavy boots and whenever she could went about bareheaded. But she was as strong as an ox and boasted that few men could drive a longer ball than she. She was plain of speech, and she could swear more variously than a stevedore. Though her name was Frances she preferred to be called Frank. Masterful, but with tact, it was her jovial strength of character that held the three together. They drank their waters together, had their baths at the same hour, they took their strenuous walks together, pounded about the tennis court with a professional to make them run, and ate at the same table their sparse and regulated meals. Nothing impaired their good humour but the scales, and when one or other of them weighed as much on one day as she had the day before neither Frank's coarse jokes, the *bonhomie* of Beatrice, nor Arrow's pretty kittenish ways sufficed to dispel the gloom. Then drastic measures were resorted to, the culprit went to bed for twenty-four hours and nothing passed her lips but the doctor's famous vegetable soup which tasted like hot water in which a cabbage had been well rinsed.

Never were three women greater friends. They would have been independent of anyone else if they had not needed a fourth at bridge. They were fierce, enthusiastic players and the moment the day's cure was over, they sat down at the bridge table. Arrow, feminine as she was, played the best game of the three, a hard, brilliant game, in which she showed no mercy and never conceded a point or failed to take advantage of a mistake. Beatrice was solid and reliable. Frank was dashing; she was a great theorist and had all the authorities at the tip of her tongue. They had long arguments over the rival systems. They bombarded one another with Culbertson and Sims. It was obvious that not one of them ever played a card without fifteen good reasons, but it was also obvious from the subsequent conversation that there were fifteen equally good reasons why she should not have played it. Life would have been perfect, even with the prospect of twenty-four hours of that filthy soup when the doctor's rotten (Beatrice) bloody (Frank) lousy (Arrow) scales pretended one hadn't lost an ounce in two days, if only there had not been this constant difficulty of finding someone to play with them who was in their class.

It was for this reason that on the occasion with which this narrative deals Frank invited Lena Finch to come and stay with them at Antibes. They were spending some weeks there on Frank's suggestion. It seemed absurd to her, with her common sense, that immediately the cure was over Beatrice who always lost twenty pounds should be giving way to her ungovernable appetite put it all on again. Beatrice was weak. She needed a person of strong will to watch her diet. She proposed then that on leaving Carlsbad they should take a house at Antibes, where they could get plenty of exercise— everyone knew that nothing slimmed you like swimming—and as far as possible could go on with the cure. With a cook of their own they could at least avoid things that were obviously fattening. There was no reason why they should not all lose several pounds more. It seemed a very good idea. Beatrice knew what was good for her, and she could resist temptation well enough if temptation was not put right under her nose. Besides, she liked gambling, and a flutter at the Casino two or three times a week would pass the time very pleasantly. Arrow adored Antibes, and she would be looking her best after a month at Carlsbad. She could just pick and choose among the young Italians, the passionate Spaniards, the gallant Frenchmen, and the long-limbed English who sauntered about all day in bathing trunks and gay-coloured dressing-gowns. The plan worked very well. They had a grand time. Two days a week they ate nothing but hard-boiled eggs and raw tomatoes and they mounted the scales every morning with light hearts. Arrow got down to eleven stone and felt just like a girl; Beatrice and Frank by standing in a certain way just avoided the thirteen. The machine they had bought registered kilogrammes, and they got extraordinarily clever at translating them in the twinkling of an eye to pounds and ounces.

But the fourth at bridge continued to be the difficulty. This person played like a fool, the other was so slow that it drove you frantic, one was quarrelsome, another was a bad loser, a third was next door to a crook. It was strange how hard it was to find exactly the player you wanted.

One morning when they were sitting in pyjamas on the terrace overlooking the sea, drinking their tea (without milk or sugar) and eating a rusk prepared by Dr Hudebert and guaranteed not to be fattening, Frank looked up from her letters.

"Lena Finch is coming down to the Riviera," she said.

"Who's she?" asked Arrow.

"She married a cousin of mine. He died a couple of months ago and she's just recovering from a nervous breakdown. What about asking her to come here for a fortnight?"

"Does she play bridge?" asked Beatrice.

"You bet your life she does," boomed Frank in her deep voice. "And a damned good game too. We should be absolutely independent of outsiders."

"How old is she?" asked Arrow.

"Same age as I am."

"That sounds all right."

It was settled. Frank, with her usual decisiveness, stalked out as soon as she had finished her breakfast to send a wire, and three days later Lena Finch arrived. Frank met her at the station. She was in

deep but not obtrusive mourning for the recent death of her husband. Frank had not seen her for two years. She kissed her warmly and took a good look at her.

"You're very thin, darling," she said.

Lena smiled bravely.

"I've been through a good deal lately. I've lost a lot of weight."

Frank sighed, but whether from sympathy with her cousin's sad loss, or from envy, was not obvious.

Lena was not, however, depressed, and after a quick bath was quite ready to accompany Frank to Eden Roc. Frank introduced the stranger to her two friends and they sat down in what was known as the Monkey House. It was an enclosure covered with glass overlooking the sea, with a bar at the back, and it was crowded with chattering people in bathing costumes, pyjamas, or dressing-gowns, who were seated at the tables having drinks. Beatrice's soft heart went out to the lorn widow, and Arrow, seeing that she was pale, quite ordinary to look at, and probably forty-eight, was prepared to like her very much. A waiter approached them.

"What will you have, Lena dear?"

Frank asked.

"Oh, I don't know, what you all have, a dry Martini or a White Lady."

Arrow and Beatrice gave her a quick look. Everyone knows how fattening cocktails are.

"I daresay you're tired after your journey," said Frank kindly.

She ordered a dry Martini for Lena and a mixed lemon and orange juice for herself and her two friends.

"We find alcohol isn't very good in all this heat," she explained.

"Oh, it never affects me at all," Lena answered airily. "I like cocktails."

Arrow went very slightly pale under her rouge (neither she nor Beatrice ever wet their faces when they bathed and they thought it absurd of Frank, a woman of her size, to pretend she liked diving) but she said nothing. The conversation was gay and easy, they all said the obvious things with gusto, and presently they strolled back to the villa for luncheon.

In each napkin were two little antifat rusks. Lena gave a bright smile as she put them by the side of her plate.

"May I have some bread?" she asked.

The grossest indecency would not have fallen on the ears of those three women with such a shock. Not one of them had eaten bread for ten years. Even Beatrice, greedy as she was, drew the line there. Frank, the good hostess, recovered herself first.

"Of course, darling," she said and turning to the butler asked him to bring some.

"And some butter," said Lena in that pleasant easy ways of hers.

There was a moment's embarrassed silence.

"I don't know if there's any in the house," said Frank, "but I'll inquire. There may be some in the kitchen."

"I adore bread and butter, don't you?" said Lena, turning to Beatrice.

Beatrice gave a sickly smile and an evasive reply. The butler brought a long crisp roll of French bread. Lena slit it in two and plastered it with the butter which was miraculously produced. A grilled sole was served.

"We eat very simply here," said Frank. "I hope you won't mind."

"Oh, no, I like my food very plain,"

said Lena as she took some butter and spread it over her fish. "As long as I can have bread and butter and potatoes and cream I'm quite happy."

The three friends exchanged a glance. Frank's great sallow face sagged a little and she looked with distaste at the dry, insipid sole on her plate. Beatrice came to the rescue.

"It's such a bore, we can't get cream here," she said. "It's one of the things one has to do without on the Riviera."

"What a pity," said Lena.

The rest of the luncheon consisted of lamb cutlets, with the fat carefully removed so that Beatrice should not be led astray, and spinach boiled in water, with stewed pears to end up with. Lena tasted her pears and gave the butler a look of inquiry. That resourceful man understood her at once and though powdered sugar had never been served at that table before handed her without a moment's hesitation a bowl of it. She helped herself liberally. The other three pretended not to notice. Coffee was served and Lena took three lumps of sugar in hers.

"You have a very sweet tooth," said

Arrow in a tone which she struggled to keep friendly.

"We think saccharine so much more sweetening," said Frank, as she put a tiny tablet of it into her coffee.

"Disgusting stuff," said Lena.

Beatrice's mouth drooped at the corners, and she gave the lump sugar a yearning look.

"Beatrice," boomed Frank sternly.

Beatrice stifled a sigh, and reached for the saccharine.

Frank was relieved when they could sit down to the bridge table. It was plain to her that Arrow and Beatrice were upset. She wanted them to like Lena and she was anxious that Lena should enjoy her fortnight with them. For the first rubber Arrow cut with the newcomer.

"Do you play Vanderbilt or Culbertson?" she asked her.

"I have no conventions," Lena answered in a happy-go-lucky way, "I play by the light of nature."

"I play strict Culbertson," said Arrow acidly.

The three fat women braced themselves to the fray. No conventions indeed!

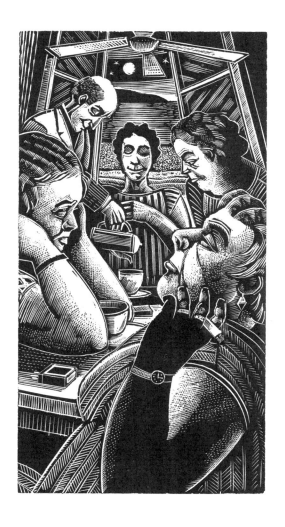

They'd learn her. When it came to bridge even Frank's family feeling was forgotten and she settled down with the same determination as the others to trim the stranger in their midst. But the light of nature served Lena very well. She had a natural gift for the game and great experience. She played with imagination, quickly, boldly, and with assurance. The other players were in too high a class not to realize very soon that Lena knew what she was about, and since they were all thoroughly good-natured, generous women, they were gradually mollified. This was real bridge. They all enjoyed themselves. Arrow and Beatrice began to feel more kindly towards Lena, and Frank, noticing this, heaved a fat sigh of relief. It was going to be a success.

After a couple of hours they parted, Frank and Beatrice to have a round of golf, and Arrow to take a brisk walk with a young Prince Roccamare whose acquaintance she had lately made. He was very sweet and young and good-looking. Lena said she would rest.

They met again just before dinner.

"I hope you've been all right, Lena

dear," said Frank. "I was rather conscience-stricken at leaving you with nothing to do all this time."

"Oh, don't apologize. I had a lovely sleep and then I went down to Juan and had a cocktail. And d'you know what I discovered? You'll be so pleased. I found a dear little tea-shop where they've got the most beautiful thick fresh cream. I've ordered half a pint to be sent every day. I thought it would be my little contribution to the household."

Her eyes were shining. She was evidently expecting them to be delighted.

"How very kind of you," said Frank, with a look that sought to quell the indignation that she saw on the faces of her two friends. "But we never eat cream. In this climate it makes one so bilious."

"I shall have to eat it all myself then," said Lena cheerfully.

"Don't you ever think of your figure?" Arrow asked with icy deliberation.

"The doctor said I must eat."

"Did he say you must eat bread and butter and potatoes and cream?"

"Yes. That's what I thought you meant when you said you had simple food."

"You'll get simply enormous," said Beatrice.

Lena laughed gaily.

"No, I shan't. You see, nothing ever makes me fat. I've always eaten everything I wanted to and it's never had the slightest effect on me."

The stony silence that followed this speech was only broken by the entrance of the butler.

"Mademoiselle est servie," he announced.

They talked the matter over late that night, after Lena had gone to bed, in Frank's room. During the evening they had been furiously cheerful, and they had chaffed one another with a friendliness that would have taken in the keenest observer. But now they dropped the mask. Beatrice was sullen, Arrow was spiteful and Frank was unmanned.

"It's not very nice for me to sit there and see her eat all the things I particularly like," said Beatrice plaintively.

"It's not very nice for any of us," Frank snapped back.

"You should never have asked her

here," said Arrow.

"How was I to know?" cried Frank.

"I can't help thinking that if she really cared for her husband she would hardly eat so much," said Beatrice. "He's only been buried two months. I mean, I think you ought to show some respect for the dead."

"Why can't she eat the same as we do?" asked Arrow viciously. "She's a guest."

"Well, you heard what she said. The doctor told her she must eat."

"Then she ought to go to a sanatorium."

"It's more than flesh and blood can stand, Frank," moaned Beatrice.

"If I can stand it you can stand it."

"She's your cousin, she's not our cousin," said Arrow. "I'm not going to sit there for fourteen days and watch that woman make a hog of herself."

"It's so vulgar to attach all this importance to food," Frank boomed, and her voice was deeper than ever. "After all the only thing that counts really is spirit."

"Are you calling *me* vulgar, Frank?" asked Arrow with flashing eyes.

"No, of course she isn't," interrupted Beatrice.

"I wouldn't put it past you to go down in the kitchen when we're all in bed and have a good square meal on the sly."

Frank sprang to her feet.

"How dare you say that, Arrow! I'd never ask anybody to do what I'm not prepared to do myself. Have you known me all these years and do you think me capable of such a mean thing?"

"How is it you never take off any weight then?"

Frank gave a gasp and burst into a flood of tears.

"What a cruel thing to say! I've lost pounds and pounds."

She wept like a child. Her vast body shook and great tears splashed on her mountainous bosom.

"Darling, I didn't mean it," cried Arrow.

She threw herself on her knees and enveloped what she could of Frank in her own plump arms. She wept and the mascara ran down her cheeks.

"D'you mean to say I don't look thinner?" Frank sobbed. "After all I've gone

through."

"Yes, dear, of course you do," cried Arrow through her tears. "Everybody's noticed it."

Beatrice, though naturally of a placid disposition, began to cry gently. It was very pathetic. Indeed, it would have been a hard heart that failed to be moved by the sight of Frank, that lion-hearted woman, crying her eyes out. Presently, however, they dried their tears and had a little brandy and water, which every doctor had told them was the least fattening thing they could drink, and then they felt much better. They decided that Lena should have the nourishing food that had been ordered her and they made a solemn resolution not to let it disturb their equanimity. She was certainly a first-rate bridge player and after all it was only for a fortnight. They would do whatever they could to make her stay enjoyable. They kissed one another warmly and separated for the night feeling strangely uplifted. Nothing should interfere with the wonderful friendship that had brought so much happiness into their three lives.

But human nature is weak. You

must not ask too much of it. They ate grilled fish while Lena ate macaroni sizzling with cheese and butter; they ate grilled cutlets and boiled spinach while Lena ate *pâté de foie gras;* twice a week they ate hard-boiled eggs and raw tomatoes, while Lena ate peas swimming in cream and potatoes cooked in all sorts of delicious ways. The chef was a good chef and he leapt at the opportunity afforded him to send up one dish more rich, tasty and succulent than the other.

"Poor Jim," sighed Lena, thinking of her husband, "he loved French cooking."

The butler disclosed the fact that he could make half a dozen kinds of cocktail and Lena informed them that the doctor had recommended her to drink burgundy at luncheon and champagne at dinner. The three fat women persevered. They were gay, chatty and even hilarious (such is the natural gift that women have for deception) but Beatrice grew limp and forlorn, and Arrow's tender blue eyes acgrew more raucous. It was when they played bridge that the strain showed itself. They had always been fond of talking over their hands, but their discussion had been friendly. Now a distinct bitterness crept in and sometimes one pointed out a mistake to another with quite unnecessary frankness. Discussion turned to argument and argument to altercation. Sometimes the session ended in angry silence. Once Frank accused Arrow of deliberately letting her down. Two or three times Beatrice, the softest of the three, was reduced to tears. On another occasion Arrow flung down her cards and swept out of the room in a pet. Their tempers were getting frayed. Lena was the peacemaker.

"I think it's such a pity to quarrel over bridge," she said. "After all, it's only a game."

It was all very well for her. She had had a square meal and half a bottle of champagne. Besides, she had phenomenal luck. She was winning all their money. The score was put down in a book after each session, and hers mounted up day after day with unfailing regularity. Was there no justice in the world? They began to hate one another. And though they hated her too they could not resist confiding in her. Each of them went to her separately and told her how detestable the others were. Arrow said she was sure it was bad for her to see so much of women so much older than herself. She had a good mind to sacrifice her share of the lease and go to Venice for the rest of the summer. Frank told Lena that with her masculine mind it was too much to expect that she could be satisfied with anyone so frivolous as Arrow and so frankly stupid as Beatrice.

"I must have intellectual conversation," she boomed. "When you have a brain like mine you've got to consort with your intellectual equals."

Beatrice only wanted peace and quiet.

"Really I hate women," she said. "They're so unreliable; they're so malicious."

By the time Lena's fortnight drew to its close the three fat women were barely on speaking terms. They kept up appearances before Lena, but when she was not there made no pretences. They had got past quarrelling. They ignored one another, and when this was not possible treated each other with icy politeness.

Lena was going to stay with friends on the Italian Riviera and Frank saw her off by the same train as that by which she arrived. She was taking away with her a lot of their money.

"I don't know how to thank you," she said, as she got into the carriage. "I've had a wonderful visit."

If there was one thing that Frank Hickson prided herself on more than on being a match for any man it was that she was a gentlewoman, and her reply was perfect in its combination of majesty and graciousness.

"We've all enjoyed having you here, Lena," she said. "It's been a real treat."

But when she turned away from the departing train she heaved such a vast sigh of relief that the platform shook beneath her. She flung back her massive shoulders and strode home to the villa.

"Ouf!" she roared at intervals. "Ouf!"

She changed into her one-piece bathing-suit, put on her espadrilles and a man's dressing-gown (no nonsense about it), and went to Eden Roc. There was still time for a bathe before luncheon. She passed through the Monkey House, look-

ing about her to say good morning to anyone she knew, for she felt on a sudden at
peace with mankind, and then stopped
dead still. She could not believe her eyes.
Beatrice was sitting at one of the tables, by
herself; she wore the pyjamas she had
bought at Molyneux's a day or two before,
she had a string of pearls round her neck,
and Frank's quick eyes saw that she had
just had her hair waved; her cheeks, her
eyes, her lips were made up. Fat, nay vast,
as she was, none could deny that she was
an extremely handsome woman. But what
was she doing? With the slouching gait of
the Neanderthal man which was Frank's
characteristic walk she went up to Beatrice. In her black bathing-dress Frank
looked like the huge cetacean which the
Japanese catch in the Torres Straits and
which the vulgar call a sea-cow.

"Beatrice, what are you doing?" she
cried in her deep voice.

It was like the roll of thunder in the
distant mountains. Beatrice looked at her
coolly.

"Eating," she answered.

"Damn it, I can see you're eating."

In front of Beatrice was a plate of

croissants and a plate of butter, a pot of strawberry jam, coffee, and a jug of cream. Beatrice was spreading butter thick on the delicious hot bread, covering this with jam, and then pouring the thick cream over all.

"You'll kill yourself," said Frank.

"I don't care," mumbled Beatrice with her mouth full.

"You'll put on pounds and pounds."

"Go to hell!"

She actually laughed in Frank's face. My God, how good those *croissants* smelt!

"I'm disappointed in you, Beatrice. I thought you had more character."

"It's your fault. That blasted woman. You would have her down. For a fortnight I've watched her gorge like a hog. It's more than flesh and blood can stand. I'm going to have one square meal if I bust."

The tears welled up to Frank's eyes. Suddenly she felt very weak and womanly. She would have liked a strong man to take her on his knee and pet her and cuddle her and call her little baby names. Speechless she sank down on a chair by Beatrice's side. A waiter came up. With a pathetic gesture she waved towards the

coffee and *croissants*.

"I'll have the same," she sighed.

She listlessly reached out her hand to take a roll, but Beatrice snatched away the plate.

"No, you don't" she said. "You wait till you get your own."

Frank called her a name which ladies seldom apply to one another in affection. In a moment the waiter brought her *croissants*, butter, jam, and coffee.

"Where's the cream, you fool?" she roared like a lioness at bay.

She began to eat. She ate gluttonously. The place was beginning to fill up with bathers coming to enjoy a cocktail or two after having done their duty by the sun and the sea. Presently Arrow strolled along with Prince Roccamare. She had on a beautiful silk wrap which she held tightly round her with one hand in order to look as slim as possible and she bore her head high so that he should not see her double chin. She was laughing gaily. She felt like a girl. He had just told her (in Italian) that her eyes made the blue of the Mediterranean look like pea-soup. He left her to go into the men's room to brush his sleek black hair and they arranged to meet in five minutes for a drink. Arrow walked on to the women's room to put a little more rouge on her cheeks and a little more red on her lips. On her way she caught sight of Frank and Beatrice. She stopped. She could hardly believe her eyes.

"My God!" she cried. "You beasts. You hogs." She seized a chair. "Waiter."

Her appointment went clean out of her head. In the twinkling of an eye the waiter was at her side.

"Bring me what these ladies are having," she ordered.

Frank lifted her great heavy head from her plate.

"Bring me some *pâté de foie gras*," she boomed.

"Frank!" cried Beatrice.

"Shut up."

"All right. I'll have some too."

The coffee was brought and the hot rolls and cream and the *pâté de foie gras* and they set to. They spread the cream on the *pâté* and they ate it. They devoured great spoonfuls of jam. They crunched the delicious crisp bread voluptuously. What was love to Arrow then? Let the Prince keep his palace in Rome and his castle in the Apennines. They did not speak. What they were about was much too serious. They ate with solemn, ecstatic fervour.

"I haven't eaten potatoes for twenty-five years," said Frank in a far-off brooding tone.

"Waiter," cried Beatrice, "bring fried potatoes for three."

"*Très bien, Madame.*"

The potatoes were brought. Not all the perfumes of Arabia smelt so sweet. They ate them with their fingers.

"Bring me a dry Martini," said Arrow.

"You can't have a dry Martini in the middle of a meal, Arrow," said Frank.

"Can't I? You wait and see."

"All right then. Bring me a double dry Martini," said Frank.

"Bring three double dry Martinis," said Beatrice.

They were brought and drunk at a gulp. The women looked at one another and sighed. The misunderstandings of the last fortnight dissolved and the sincere affection each had for the others welled up again in their hearts. They could hardly believe that they had ever contemplated the possibility of severing a friendship that had brought them so much solid satisfaction. They finished the potatoes.

"I wonder if they've got any chocolate éclairs," said Beatrice.

"Of course they have."

And of course they had. Frank thrust one whole into her huge mouth, swallowed it and seized another, but before she ate it she looked at the other two and plunged a vindictive dagger into the heart of the monstrous Lena.

"You can say what you like, but the truth is she played a damned rotten game of bridge, really."

"Lousy," agreed Arrow.

But Beatrice suddenly thought she would like a meringue.

W. SOMERSET MAUGHAM

WHEN MAUGHAM DIED IN 1965 AT the age of 91, he was generally recognized as the grand old man of English letters. And rightly so. As playwright, novelist, essayist, and especially short-story writer, he had entertained and enlightened the reading world for over half a century.

Every Maugham play and story is cleverly crafted, with a distinct beginning, middle, and end, and many depend upon plot twists that are often barely believable. Maugham, the consummate story-teller, used these conventional devices so deftly that his literary voice—elegant, urbane, ironic—continues to appeal.